THE GHOST IN ROOM 11

THE GHOST IN ROOM 11

Betty Ren Wright

illustrated by Jacqueline Rogers

SCHOLASTIC INC.

New York Toronto London Auckland Sydney
Mexico City New Delhi Hong Kong Buenos Aires

ISBN 0-439-54652-4

Published by Scholastic Inc., 557 Broadway, New York, NY 10012,
by arrangement with Holiday House, Inc.
SCHOLASTIC and associated logos are trademarks
and/or registered trademarks of Scholastic Inc.

12 11 10 9 8 7   7 8/0

Printed in the U.S.A.   40

First Scholastic printing, March 2003

For Dorothy Tofte with my love

CONTENTS

1. "This School Is Haunted!" 1
2. A Bunch of Lies 8
3. Hiding in the Closet 14
4. "You Saw—*What?*" 19
5. The Picture in the Hall 23
6. Going to Room 11 28
7. "Ghost Man" 37
8. A Famous Friend 42
9. "Shocking" 47
10. "The Ghost in Room Eleven" 52
11. Trouble at Home 62
12. The Ghost Hunt 66
13. Bad Days Ahead 72
14. "I'll Haunt You Forever!" 76
15. Two Miracles 82
16. A Celebration 87
17. "You Could Be Killed!" 92
18. Cleaning up the Mess 99
19. The Ghost Appears 102
20. Thumbs up for Miss Whipple 109

THE GHOST IN ROOM 11

1

"This School Is Haunted!"

MATT BARBER SAT, hunched over, on a swing and dug one heel into the dirt. He was the only person left on the school playground. He might even be the only person left in the world. What if a poison cloud were drifting across the town of Healy right now? What if the birds started to drop out of the trees, and that ant crawling across the gravel rolled over on its back and. . . .

He shivered and gave himself a little push. It was no fun starting in a new school a month late. The kids at Healy Elementary had known each other since they were babies. They weren't interested in a new kid from the big city.

Think about tomorrow, he told himself. Tomorrow he was going to give a speech in front of his new fourth grade, and after that, everybody would know who he was.

"I'm not supposed to talk about this, but I'm going to anyway." He said the words out loud to get used to them. "I'm going to tell you about my real mother and father. My real mother does stunts in the movies. Once she jumped from a twelve-story building and landed in a pond about as big as a bathtub." He frowned. Maybe a bathtub was too small. "About as big as *two* bathtubs, only a lot deeper. And once she drove a car off a cliff and blew it up before it landed."

Cool, he thought. *That's cool!*

"My real dad is a treasure hunter. He dives down to old wrecks, and when he finds treasure he gets to keep it. Sometimes he sends me a souvenir." When he said that, he was going to hold up the gold piece Uncle Jim had sent him as a joke, along with a book about treasure hunting. It wasn't a real gold piece, but that didn't matter.

It would fool everybody in this dumb country school.

He paused, wondering what his teacher, Mrs. Sanders, would think of his speech. She had said you could talk about anything, as long as the subject was important to you. Well, parents were important, weren't they?

"My real mom does dangerous stuff every day—that's why she let me be adopted. She didn't want to, but she thought she might get killed or something. Next summer my real dad is going to take me to Mexico—"

The school door burst open, and three boys tumbled out, laughing and pushing one another. Matt slid off the swing, but not fast enough. The boys raced across the yard and stopped in front of him.

"I guess that's what kids do in Milwaukee." Charlie Peck chuckled. "They play with babies' toys."

Matt clenched his fists. He hated being laughed at. His dad would probably say Charlie was just kidding, but his dad would be wrong. Everyone at Healy Elementary was mean.

"I wasn't playing," Matt said. "I was wishing I was back at my old school. If I was, I'd be swimming right now."

Charlie's eyes widened. "Your school had a swimming pool? I don't believe it."

"Who cares whether you believe it or not?" Matt backed up, eager to get away.

"What else did you have in that school?"

"Two gyms," Matt said, "one for boys and one for girls. And an auditorium with a real stage." The auditorium part was true. "And we had a big cafeteria where we could get pizza or anything else we wanted. Every day!" He stopped, aware that he'd gone too far.

"Sure!" Charlie laughed, and the other boys laughed, too. "Boy, pizza every day! That's a joke!" They started to move off, but then Charlie came back.

"I bet Healy has one thing your big-city school doesn't have," he said slyly.

"Like what?" Matt glanced at the long, low school building. It looked like a prison.

"We have a ghost!" Charlie said. "This school is haunted, believe it or not."

"Not," Matt said. "There's no such thing as a ghost."

"Sure there is!" Charlie insisted. "This is an old school, and it's haunted. Ask the teachers. Ask Mr. Beasley."

Mr. Beasley was the principal. Matt had met him on his first day at Healy. He'd told Matt that the governor of the state and the mayor of Healy had been students at Healy Elementary. He'd talked about hard work and no shoving in the halls. He hadn't said a word about ghosts.

"Or if you're scared to ask Mr. Beasley," Charlie went on, "you can find out for yourself."

"How?" Matt asked, not really wanting to know.

"Hide in the school till everybody leaves. See what happens."

Matt wished he'd gone home instead of hanging around the playground. Being alone in a new house was no fun, but talking to Charlie was even worse.

"Why would I want to be stuck in school all night?" he said nervously. "My folks would call the police."

"You wouldn't be stuck," Charlie argued. "You can always open the front door from the inside."

Matt started toward the road, walking fast. "Only stupid people believe in ghosts," he yelled over his shoulder. "Ghosts are stupid!"

He felt better after that, but only for a minute. Then he realized he'd left his library book next to the swing. He whirled around, but Charlie already had the book in his hand.

"Forget something?" he teased.

Matt grabbed it and ran across the playground with *Fifteen Famous Ghost Stories* clutched in his hand. He tried not to hear the laughter that followed him.

Just wait, he thought, but he didn't know what he meant. He only knew that moving to Healy was the worst thing that had ever happened to him.

2

A Bunch of Lies

"So HOW IS IT GOING at school?" Matt's dad asked that evening. "Are you making friends?"

Matt shrugged. "It's okay." He kept his eyes on the television and hoped his mother wasn't listening. She could tell when he was hiding something.

"If people aren't friendly, it may be your own fault," she called now, from the kitchen. "Try hard, Matthew. Smile. You have a very nice smile."

Matt sank deeper in his chair. Could his mother read other people's minds the way she read his?

Luckily, his dad couldn't read minds at all. "Well, I'm glad you're off to a good start," he said. "Healy is a fine place to grow up in." He switched channels, but Matt didn't care. The sooner they stopped talking about school the better. No one else knew what it was like, being the new kid.

The next morning the Barbers left the house together. His parents drove to the bus station, and Matt walked down the road toward the school. When he was close enough to hear voices from the playground, he sat under a tree.

Big-mouth Charlie, he thought. After today things would be different. After his speech, everyone in the class would know Matt Barber was special.

He stayed under the tree until he heard the warning bell. Then he ran, leaning forward with his arms spread like Superman. He reached the school door just in time to file in with the rest of the fourth grade.

Matt's seat was in the back row, which could be either good or bad. It was good because most of the time Mrs. Sanders seemed to forget he was there. It was bad when she remembered. Today it was very bad, because the first thing she did was return yesterday's spelling tests.

"You and I are going to have to do some hard work, Matthew," she said. "I almost wore out my pencil on this one." She laid the test on Matt's desk. There were fifteen words on the list, and twelve of them had checks next to them. Some kids giggled.

"Don't you dare laugh," Mrs. Sanders said sternly. "There wasn't a perfect paper in the whole class. I'm ashamed of all of you! Your homework tonight will be to write each misspelled word ten times."

Later, when it was time to start their speeches, Mrs. Sanders called on Matt first. "I'm sure you have something interesting to tell us," she said. Matt guessed she was sorry she'd made the class laugh at him.

He didn't smile back. His legs moved jerkily as he walked to the front of the room. When he turned to face the class, he couldn't remember one word of what he'd planned to say. Then he glanced at Charlie Peck. Charlie snickered, and the snicker made Matt remember.

"I'm not supposed to talk about this," he began, "but I'm going to anyway."

The words were like magic. The kids stopped wriggling. Charlie's grin faded. Mrs. Sanders looked as if she wanted to say something, but didn't.

Matt cleared his throat. "I'm going to tell you about my real mother and father." For just one second he pictured his real mom and dad, and he felt guilty. But they were at work in Milwaukee, and he was here. Last night his mother had said it was his own fault if he didn't make friends. She'd said he had to try hard. *Okay*, he thought, *I'm trying.*

"My real mom does stunts in the movies. . . . My real father is a treasure hunter." He told about some of the stunts his mother did, including some new ones he'd made up in bed last night. He held up the "gold piece."

Matt hoped the class would clap when he finished, but they didn't. They just looked at him.

Mrs. Sanders asked if anyone wanted to comment on the talk.

"It was a bunch of lies," Charlie said.

"That's enough," Mrs. Sanders said sharply. "You're being rude, Charles."

"Matt talked in a nice loud voice," Stephanie James said, after a moment.

"That's better," Mrs. Sanders said. "I hope everyone else will speak as clearly as Matthew did."

Nobody said, "You're lucky to have such great parents, Matthew." When Matt walked back to his seat, no one looked at him, except Stephanie. She smiled as if she were sorry for him.

There were four more talks that day, but Matt didn't hear a word of them. He kept trying to figure out what had gone wrong. It was Charlie's fault, he decided. Charlie had called him a liar. He wished a bolt of lightning would shoot through the open window and hit Charlie. It could hit all of them, except Stephanie.

At recess he told Mrs. Sanders he wanted to stay inside and read, but she wouldn't let him. Charlie waited with his pals outside the door.

"You are the biggest liar I ever heard," Charlie said. "You make up stuff all the time, and you're a chicken besides. All you can do is talk."

Matt took a step backward. "I'm not a chicken," he said. "My real mother's going to teach me to do stunts someday. I'm not afraid of anything."

Charlie looked sideways at the other boys. "Prove it," he said. Matt saw that he'd stepped into a trap. "Stay after school tonight and watch for the ghost. I bet you're too chicken to do that."

"No, I'm not," Matt said, because there was nothing else he could say. "I'll do it. Big deal."

He looked up, hoping again for a bolt of lightning. This time he wished it would crash down on his own head. He wanted to disappear in a flash of light and never come back.

That would wipe the grin off Charlie Peck's face.

3

Hiding in the Closet

"It's DOWN THERE at the bottom of the stairs."
Charlie gave Matt a push. "Hurry up! Hide!"

Matt looked longingly at the door to the playground. The few students left in the school were heading out, and there wasn't a single teacher in sight. Where were they when you needed them?

"What if a janitor comes to get a mop or something?"

"The cleaning stuff is stored up here," Charlie said. "There's nothing in that closet except books.

Unless the ghost hides in there," he added. "Who knows?"

Matt glared at him and thumped down the stairs. The basement was cool and dim with doors in every direction. They could lead to cells, Matt thought, like a dungeon in a castle. He stopped at the door Charlie had pointed out. Maybe it would be locked. He glanced over his shoulder and saw Charlie watching from the top of the stairs as he turned the knob. The door opened, and there was nothing to do but step inside.

He looked around. Boxes lined the closet walls. Overhead there was a long shelf that held a fan, a globe, and more boxes. The room smelled musty.

"Close the door!" Charlie called softly. "Someone's coming."

Matt pulled the door shut and leaned against a stack of boxes. Someone shouted upstairs. Heels clicked along the corridor. A voice said, "See you tomorrow." Finally there were no sounds at all.

Charlie had said the janitors would leave after an hour. Matt wondered how he could be sure they were gone? Time passed slowly in the dark.

He sank down, cross-legged, on the floor and

waited. The beginning of a sneeze tickled his nose. His eyes ached from staring at nothing.

He may have fallen asleep; he wasn't sure. But suddenly he was wide awake, certain that he was no longer alone. Something was moving, close by.

The sound grew louder. It came from overhead, Matt realized, up on the shelf. He pictured a tiny mouse and he felt better, but only for a second. It could just as easily be a big, ugly rat. Or a bat! Or a huge, hairy tarantula like the one he'd seen on television last week.

With a yelp, he scrambled to his feet and fumbled for the doorknob. The rustling grew louder. He found the knob, hurtled out into the basement, and raced up the stairs.

The hallway looked different in the shadows of late afternoon. The only light came through the glass panes of the classroom doors along the hall. Matt started toward the playground and then froze. Footsteps sounded from the far end of the hall. Someone was still in the building.

The footsteps were slow and loud. Matt wondered how he could hear them so clearly, when all the classroom doors were closed.

He pressed himself against a locker and tried to decide what to do. If he ran to the playground door, the person might come out of a classroom and see him. If he stayed where he was, he would be caught for sure. If he ran back to the closet— *no!* The bat-rat-spider was waiting for him there.

He blinked. The hall seemed to grow longer, stretching toward a pinpoint of light that widened into a silvery cloud as he stared. A tall woman in a black dress came out of the last classroom. *A teacher*, Matt thought. She raised a hand and beckoned.

Matt edged along the row of lockers, his eyes on the woman. He didn't know what to do. Then he saw something that made his stomach do flip-flops. The door to the last classroom was still closed. The woman had walked right through it.

"MATTHEW BARBER!" The words echoed down the hall.

Until that minute Matt hadn't believed Charlie's story that the school was haunted. But now he had seen for himself. There really was a ghost in Healy Elementary—and she knew his name.

4

"You Saw—What?"

Matt was a fast runner. Back in Milwaukee, he could beat every kid in his class. But now, he felt as if he were hardly moving. Any second, a hand was going to close on his shoulder. A terrifying voice was going to roar, "MATTHEW BARBER!" into his ear.

As he dashed across the playground, he thought he heard giggles, but he didn't stop. If Charlie and his friends were watching, maybe the ghost would catch *them*. It would serve them right!

When he turned onto Graylog Lane the station wagon was in the drive. His father looked up in surprise as Matt staggered into the kitchen.

"Slow down, boy. What's the big rush?"

"Where's Mom?" Matt gasped. He slumped into a chair. "I've got to tell you something."

"I'm here," his mother said from the hall. "And I've just had an unpleasant surprise! We've been here only a month, and your teacher is already calling. Mrs. Sanders says you are one of the worst spellers she's had."

Matt hardly heard her. "Something awful happened," he said. "I saw a—"

"And that's not all," his mother interrupted. "She told me about the speech you gave today."

"Oh." Matt looked away. "It was just . . . a speech. Everybody has to give one."

"But I'll bet everyone didn't pick such an unusual subject. Matthew told the class about his real parents," she explained to Matt's dad. "His *real* father is a deep-sea diver who hunts for treasure. His *real* mother is a stuntwoman in the movies."

There was a long silence. "I don't even know how to swim," Matt's father said.

"It was just a speech," Matt repeated. "I would have told the truth later on."

"You mean the truth about your plain old bank teller mother and salesman father?" his mom asked. She turned again to his dad. "Matthew's *real* mother drove off a cliff and blew up the car on the way down."

"Amazing," his dad said. "I bet she makes a lot of money doing that."

Matt looked from one of them to the other. They were laughing, but he could tell they were sort of hurt.

"Mrs. Sanders said the other children didn't believe you," his mom said. "She heard them talking."

"It wasn't lying exactly," Matt said. "It was just—"

"It was lying," his mother said firmly. "You were trying to impress people, and it didn't work."

Matt's dad reached over and gave him a tap on the arm. "No more stories, right? Now let's forget it. You have something important to tell us. You saw—what?"

Matt swallowed hard. *I saw a ghost in school. She called my name.* He imagined the look on his mother's face if he told them that.

"Well," his mother said impatiently, "what did you see?"

Matt stood up. "Nothing," he said. "I forgot."

It was weird, telling another lie, when he wanted more than anything to tell the truth.

5

The Picture in the Hall

"WHAT'S THE GHOST look like?" Jason Myers asked the next morning. Jason was Charlie's best friend.

Matt pretended not to hear. He wasn't going to talk about the ghost. His parents wouldn't believe him, and his classmates had already decided he was a liar. Besides, he was pretty sure the boys didn't believe there was a ghost; they had just wanted to play a trick on him. He was sure of it when Charlie came up the basement stairs carrying a cage with two gerbils in it.

Jason grinned at Matt. "Charlie's speech is about how to take care of gerbils," he said.

So that was what had been rustling on the closet shelf!

All morning long Matt tried to decide what to do. He could run away, but where would he go? If he took the bus to Milwaukee, he could call Jerry or Mike or Paul—but their parents would call his parents. He'd be back in Healy in no time.

He was glad when recess arrived. The students lined up and filed out of the room. Matt gave one quick look down the hall, to the spot where the ghost had appeared. The fifth graders were there, with their teacher, Miss Carey. She was short and round with red hair—nothing like the tall, terrifying figure he'd seen the night before.

Matt headed toward the door. Then, to his horror, he saw the ghost, peering at him from a gold frame above a row of lockers. He stepped back and stumbled over a foot. When he turned around, Mr. Beasley was brushing off his shoes.

"I—I was looking at the picture," Matt stammered.

Mr. Beasley nodded. "Miss Edna Whipple," he said solemnly. "She was already famous here at Healy when I entered kindergarten. They say she died at her desk, correcting papers." He sounded as if he thought that was a fine way to die.

Matt stared at the picture. *Miss Edna Whipple*, he thought. She had known Matt's name, and now he knew hers.

"That was Miss Whipple's motto." Mr. Beasley pointed to a gold plate at the bottom of the frame. It read: *Try Hard. Then Try Harder.*

"A good motto," Mr. Beasley said. "You might start by trying harder to stay in the line, Matthew."

A moment later Matt was out in the sunshine. He stood there, glad to escape Miss Whipple's glare.

"I'm sorry Charlie played a trick on you." Stephanie was beside him. "I don't blame you for running away. I would have been scared, too."

"I wasn't running away from those stupid gerbils," Matt said crossly. "It was something else."

"What else?" Stephanie wanted to know. "There isn't any ghost, you know. It's just a story."

"I don't want to talk about it," Matt told her.

"Do you want to play ball or something?"

She felt sorry for him! Matt wanted to punch her—or Charlie, or Jason, or even Mr. Beasley. He was more mixed-up than he'd ever been before.

"I've got stuff to do," he said. He walked off toward the edge of the playground and left Stephanie standing alone.

6

Going to Room 11

"A SLEEP OVER at school!" Matt's mother was reading the school newsletter. "What an unusual idea! Why didn't you tell us about it, Matthew?"

"Because it's dumb," Matt said. "Who wants to sleep at school?"

His mom frowned. "This will be a good chance for you to make some friends," she told him. "It says here that the fourth, fifth, and sixth grades are invited. They've got all kinds of fun things planned."

"I'm not going," Matt said. "I'm allergic to that school." But he knew he'd have to go. When his mother got that look on her face, she always had her way.

Thursday evening, his dad came home with a big package that turned out to be a bright red sleeping bag. "First choice among smart fourth graders!" he kidded, as Matt tore off the wrappings.

Matt thought red looked babyish, but he didn't say so. He had something worse to worry about. How could he spend a whole night in school, knowing Miss Whipple was hiding somewhere, watching him?

When Friday evening arrived, his mother and father insisted on taking him to school before going out to dinner. They even came in with him.

The sleep over was in the gym. Tables of snacks were set along the wall, and most of the floor was covered with sleeping bags. There were air mattresses, too, and patio lounges. Matt was surprised to see a few parents sitting around in bathrobes and slippers.

"Where do you want your sleeping bag?" Matt's dad asked. "Might as well put it close to your friends."

Matt stared at the floor.

"Matthew," his mother said, "the way to have a friend is to be a friend. Isn't that Charles Peck over there? His mother takes the same bus we do every morning."

Mrs. Sanders saved Matt from answering. She hurried up to say hello to his parents, looking very different in her blue robe and fuzzy slippers.

"Good for you, Matthew," she said cheerfully. "I'm glad you're here. You'll have a great time."

Not a chance, Matt thought. He picked up his sleeping bag and headed across the gym. A T.V. in one corner was playing a video about elephants. No one was watching it. He dropped his sleeping bag in front of the screen and sat with his back to the rest of the room.

Pretend you're home, he told himself.

It worked for a while, but then he heard Mrs. Sanders calling from the other end of the gym. "Everybody, gather around. Marco the Magician has come to entertain us."

30

Matthew stared at the elephants.

"Everybody! Right *now!*"

Matt turned around, just as a man in a black suit and cape swept into the gym. The man bowed to Mrs. Sanders and to the students. Then he reached down and picked up a blanket that had been folded on an air mattress.

"Pardon me, miss," he said to the girl sitting on the mattress. "You're not supposed to bring pets in here."

"I didn't—" the girl began, but before she could finish, Marco lifted a corner of the blanket and pulled out a white rabbit. Then he scooped up the girl's pillow and pulled a wriggling snake from the pillowcase. Everyone screamed.

Matt joined the circle just as the magician grabbed Jason by the shoulder and pretended to shake him.

"You're no better than she is!" he scolded. He drew another snake from Jason's pajama top.

For the next half hour Marco did card tricks, made balls disappear, and poured cherry soda from an empty pitcher. When the magician borrowed Mr. Beasley's glasses and made them disappear too, everyone cheered except Mr. Beasley.

"Are you sure I didn't give them back to you?" Marco asked. He sounded worried. Mr. Beasley shook his head.

"Are you very sure?" Marco repeated. "What's that in your bathrobe pocket?"

It was the glasses, of course. Mr. Beasley looked relieved and everybody clapped as Marco bowed and whirled his cape around him.

After that there were snacks, and then a ventriloquist. The ventriloquist knew about a million riddles, but his dummy couldn't answer any of them. Pretty soon Matt and the rest of the audience were shouting out the answers. By the time a delivery man came in with a stack of pizza boxes, they were starving.

Several of the teachers and parents put the pizza slices on paper plates. Miss Carey, the fifth-grade teacher, handed out the plates.

"When you finish eating, I'm sure most of you will be ready to sleep," she said. "But for those who are still wide awake, I have a very scary video I think you'll like. If you want to see it, take your plates and go to the T.V."

About twenty kids headed to the corner, Matt included. He didn't want to watch a scary video, not in Healy School. But his sleeping bag was in front of the T.V. He'd have to find another place for it.

The students settled down in front of the T.V., while Matthew dragged his sleeping bag to one side.

"Hi." It was Miss Carey, her round face pinker than ever. "Would you do me a favor? I thought I had the video in my purse, but I must have left it on my desk. Will you run down and get it, please?"

Matt dropped the bedroll and stared at her in horror. "Which—which room is yours?"

Miss Carey looked surprised. "Oh, you're the new boy, aren't you? Well, it's easy to find Room Eleven. It's at the end of the hall. You can't get lost."

Matt's stomach churned, and he wondered if he was going to throw up. He wanted to say no, but Miss Carey was already telling the other students that Matthew had offered to get the video, and they would start as soon as he returned.

Offered! What a joke! Matt's feet felt like lead as he edged around the sleepers on the floor.

"Hurry, please," Miss Carey called softly, so as not to wake anyone. "We're waiting for you."

Matt opened the gym door and looked down the hall toward Room 11. Bands of moonlight streamed in from the classrooms between the hulking rows of lockers. He shuddered and let the gym door close.

It was like stepping into a nightmare. Matt moved slowly down the hall. When he reached the front door, he stopped. One glimpse of that silver cloud, he promised himself, and he'd run right out the door and head for home. Miss Carey would be angry and worried, and the kids would say he was crazy, but it wouldn't matter. They had never seen the ghost of Miss Whipple. They didn't know.

He walked on, even more slowly than before. The hall was empty. He passed Room 10 and

looked back at the streak of light that marked the door to the gym. It was far away.

Just a few more steps. . . .

Maybe, he thought, the ghost had returned to wherever ghosts came from. Or maybe she was busy scaring someone else. With trembling fingers he reached for the doorknob of Room 11 and peeked through the glass panes.

Miss Whipple was staring back at him. She was right there, inches away, her dark eyes glittering in a face that looked as if it were carved from ice. As Matt stared, unable to move, she lifted a bony finger and beckoned. The doorknob moved under his hand.

7

"Ghost Man"

MATT RACED DOWN THE HALL so fast his feet hardly seemed to touch the floor. *Don't let her follow me*, he prayed. He didn't dare look back.

When he burst into the gym, most of the kids were asleep. In the far corner, Miss Carey and the group of video watchers waited, looking bored.

Matt tiptoed to the corner. "I—I couldn't find it," he whispered hoarsely. "I'm sorry."

Miss Carey looked puzzled. "Well, I suppose I'll have to go myself," she said. "But I don't understand why—oh, my, you're pale! Are you all right?"

"I'm okay." Matt watched the teacher make her way to the gym door. He knew he should warn her, but he was too scared to leave the safety of the corner.

"Hey, what's the matter, Barber?" Jason Myers sneered. "You look as if you're going to cry."

Matt gulped. "Nothing's the matter," he snapped. He climbed into his sleeping bag and watched the door.

It seemed a long time before Miss Carey came back. "It was in a drawer," she said. "I was sure I'd left it out—sorry."

Matt crawled deeper into his sleeping bag. Why hadn't she seen the ghost? There was only one answer, and it was a frightening one. The ghost of Miss Whipple appeared to Matthew Barber and nobody else.

For the hundredth time he wished he was back in Milwaukee. Maybe his old school didn't have sleep overs, but it wasn't haunted, either.

"I'm sure you haven't slept at all." Matt's mother smiled as he came into the kitchen the next morning and dropped his sleeping bag. "You have the sleep-over look."

Matt nodded. She was right—he'd hardly slept all night. When he did doze off, he was right back in that nightmare hallway, walking toward Room 11.

"You'll probably be asleep in ten minutes," his mother teased. "You'll be dead to the world for hours."

"I don't want to sleep." If he closed his eyes, he knew he'd see Miss Whipple's face peering out of the dark.

He wished he could talk to someone about what had happened last night. But there was no one, he thought unhappily. Then he remembered the girl who'd said she was sorry Charlie had played a joke on him. Stephanie might believe him. He wondered where she lived.

All that morning, while he carried out garbage and cleaned his room, Matt kept thinking about Miss Whipple. What if she could leave Healy Elementary when she wanted to? What if she started haunting him at home?

"Run downstairs and get the clothes from the

dryer," his mother said. Then she shook her head. "Oh, never mind. Go upstairs and take a nap."

Matt didn't want to go upstairs, any more than he wanted to go down to the basement.

"I'm not sleepy," he said. "Maybe I should dig up some weeds."

"Not until your dad comes back from town," his mother replied. "You don't know a weed from a watermelon." But she didn't stop him when he wandered outside.

It was a warm, sunny day—not a day to see a ghost, Matt told himself. He walked up the driveway and started along the road to the school. The kids played softball there on Saturday afternoons. He'd heard them setting up teams every Friday.

Maybe Stephanie would be at the playground with the others.

He stopped in a grove of trees at the edge of the playground. A game had started, and some little kids were playing on the swings. He didn't see Stephanie.

"Hey, it's the ghost hunter!" Charlie Peck, in

the outfield, was pointing at him. The whole team started to laugh.

Matt ducked deeper into the woods.

"Hey, ghost man, come on out!" shouted another voice.

Matt stayed in the woods until the kids forgot about him. It didn't take long. Then he went home, feeling lonelier than he ever had in his life.

Music floated from the windows of his house, and the leaves of the crabapple tree danced in the breeze. He looked at the hammock his father had set up under the tree. Maybe if he lay down for a couple of minutes, out here in the warm, safe sunshine. . . . He tumbled into the hammock and was asleep almost at once.

It was after five when his dad woke him. "Time for dinner, sleepyhead." He grinned down at Matt. "You've slept away a whole beautiful Saturday afternoon. That's what happens when you stay up all night having fun!"

8

A Famous Friend

"QUIET, CLASS!" Mrs. Sanders clapped her hands.

Matt jumped. He was scared all the time now. If anything really frightening happened, he'd fly apart in a thousand pieces.

"We're going to have a contest," Mrs. Sanders announced. "The fifth and sixth grades are going to take part, too. It's a writing contest—either a true story or one you've made up. Miss Bucher, our librarian, and her helpers will pick the winners."

"What're the prizes?" Charlie wanted to know.

"The two winners will read their stories at an assembly. And there will be someone famous here to listen. Merry Monahan, the author, is coming to visit us."

"Cool!" Some of the boys and girls clapped. Even Charlie looked impressed.

"She's coming as a special favor," Mrs. Sanders went on. "She's an old friend of Matthew's mother."

Matt jumped again. His mother had never mentioned that she knew a famous author.

"You're lucky!" Stephanie whispered. Matt wondered if Mrs. Sanders had made a mistake.

"I'm going to write about crossing Lake Michigan on the ferry," Stephanie said in a low voice. "My sister got seasick and we both got sunburned, and I almost fell over the railing. It was really fun. What about you?"

"Don't know." As long as Matt had Miss Whipple to worry about, a contest didn't seem important. Besides, writing meant spelling. He had enough trouble keeping up with the daily spelling tests.

When he got home that afternoon, Matt made

a sandwich and went out to the hammock. The bus from Milwaukee reached Healy at five-thirty, and the drive from the bus station took five minutes, unless his parents stopped for groceries. When he'd eaten his sandwich, he lay back and stared up at the sky. Birds had an easy life, he thought—nothing to be afraid of but cats.

It was nearly six when the station wagon turned into the drive. Matt rolled out of the hammock.

"Do you really know Merry Monahan?" he demanded, as his mother stepped out of the car. "Mrs. Sanders said so."

His mom smiled. "Don't be so surprised, Matthew," she said. "We were roommates in college, and I just happened to run into her at lunch a couple of weeks ago. I didn't know she had become a writer, but she told me all about it."

"We're supposed to write stories because she's coming," Matt complained. "I don't have anything to write about."

His dad handed him a bag of groceries. "Write about something you know," he suggested.

"That's a good idea," Matt's mother agreed.

"Write about what it feels like to leave your old friends and have to make new ones. Tell the truth, Matthew. It'll help the other students understand you."

Matt took a banana from the grocery bag and wandered down the hall to his bedroom. He thought about what his parents had said. *Tell the truth—it'll help the other students understand you. Write about something you know.* The words bounced around with a message all their own. Suddenly he knew what it was.

If there wasn't one single person he could tell about Miss Whipple, then maybe he ought to tell everybody! He could write about what happened the night he hid in the closet, and what had happened at the sleep over. He could tell the truth. People might believe him, and they might not, *but they wouldn't be sure.* He'd be the boy who might have seen a ghost.

He could hardly wait to start writing.

9

"Shocking"

"Do you want to stay after school and play T-ball with us?" Stephanie asked one afternoon.

Matt shook his head. He was working on his story every evening. If it was good enough, Stephanie wouldn't have to feel sorry for him much longer.

The story was taking a long time to finish. He wrote about how some boys had dared him to look for a ghost. He told about the noises in the closet and about seeing Charlie bring the gerbil cage up from the closet the next day. He put down how he had run upstairs and had seen the cloud of silvery light.

Describing Miss Whipple was hard. Just thinking about her made Matt feel sick. She was tall and thin, and she wore a black dress. Her skin was paper-white, and her eyes—he couldn't find the right words for her eyes. Her glare had been terrifying when he'd seen her at the end of the hall. It had been a thousand times worse when he'd peeked through the glass into Room 11 and found her looking back at him from the other side.

As he finished each paragraph, Matt stopped to look up the words he wasn't sure of. Most of the time he'd spelled them wrong. He wished his parents would get a spell-check program for the computer, but they said he shouldn't depend on a machine to do the hard work.

"I have everybody's story but yours, Matthew," Mrs. Sanders said a few days later. "You must turn it in tomorrow. Miss Bucher wants to get started reading."

"It's just about finished," Matt told her. That night he read what he'd written, and the story made him shiver. He hoped it would make Miss Bucher shiver, too.

After dinner he did math problems, and then he wrote the words he'd had wrong on that day's spelling test. When he'd copied each word ten times, it was time for his Mystery Theater. He forgot all about studying the list of words for tomorrow's spelling test.

"Honestly, Matthew!" Mrs. Sanders exclaimed the next afternoon. "I think you're getting worse instead of better. You'd better stay after school today and write all your misspelled words *twenty* times instead of ten."

Matt looked at her pleadingly. "I can think better at home," he said.

Mrs. Sanders shook her head. "Here," she said.

At three-fifteen Matt watched glumly as the rest of the fourth graders filed out. Ten words, he thought, twenty times each. Two hundred words to finish before he could leave!

He began to write furiously.

"I'm going to the office, Matthew," Mrs.

Sanders said, after about twenty minutes. "I'll be right back."

Matt's hands grew clammy. He wrote faster. Seven columns of words were finished. Eight. Nine. His fingers ached from clenching his pencil, but he didn't dare slow down. What if Mrs. Sanders decided to go home and made him stay, by himself, until he'd finished?

What if she'd already left?

Why was the room so quiet?

He turned around. There, just behind his left shoulder, stood Miss Whipple. She was close enough for him to see the shiny black buttons on her dress and to feel her icy breath as she bent over his desk.

A long white finger tapped his paper. "Shocking!" she said in a harsh whisper. "Can't you do *anything* right?"

Matt tried to yell, but he couldn't. He tried to slide out the other side of his seat, but he couldn't. For what seemed an endless time, Miss Whipple glared down at him. Then footsteps broke the silence. Miss Whipple vanished as Mrs. Sanders came through the door.

"Daydreaming again, Matthew?" she asked. "Have you finished all the words?"

Matt carried his paper up to her desk, looking over his shoulder all the way. He was ready to dive right through a window if Miss Whipple appeared again.

"Oh, Matthew, it's 'phantom' not 'panthom,'" Mrs. Sanders said crossly. She pointed at the same word the ghost had pointed at. "Do you know what a phantom is?"

Matt cleared his throat. "It's a g-g-ghost."

Mrs. Sanders looked up from his paper. "Goodness gracious!" she said. "You're absolutely green! You look as if you've seen a phantom yourself. But that's not likely, is it?" She waited, but Matt didn't say anything. "You'd better go home and get a good night's sleep."

Her words stayed in Matt's head like a bad joke, as he raced out of the school. He'd probably never get a good night's sleep again—not when he knew Miss Whipple might be waiting in his dreams to whisper "Shocking!" in his ear.

10

"The Ghost in Room Eleven"

"MATTHEW, you surprise me!"

Matt was stuffing his jacket into his locker when Mrs. Sanders stopped beside him. She stared at him for a moment, and then walked on, shaking her head.

"She was carrying our stories!" Stephanie said excitedly. "Maybe you won! I hope we both won!"

"It's not such a big deal," Matt muttered. But his heart was thumping. He wondered if Mrs.

Sanders was surprised because his story was so terrific!

The pile of papers stayed on Mrs. Sanders's desk all day, under her green frog paperweight. By three o'clock Matt thought he must have looked at the frog about a thousand times.

At ten minutes after three, Mrs. Sanders finally moved the frog and picked up the stories.

"Miss Bucher and her helpers have chosen two winners of the story contest," she said.

Matt held his breath.

"Our winner is—" She looked up and down the rows of desks, teasingly. "One winner is 'The Ghost in Room Eleven,' written by our very own Matthew Barber."

Nobody made a sound until Mrs. Sanders started to clap. Then the class clapped, too.

"Is it true or made-up?" Charlie demanded.

"You can decide that yourself at the assembly tomorrow," Mrs. Sanders replied. "I think you'll agree that he's done a fine piece of work. Except for the spelling, Matthew. We'll talk about the spelling later."

Matt's smile faded, but only for a second. He'd won!

After school, Charlie and Jason followed him across the playground.

"You should have put my name on that story instead of yours," Charlie said. "I gave you the idea."

Matt kept on walking.

"Well, I did, didn't I?" Charlie insisted. "I told you there was a ghost, and you made up a story. Right?"

"Wait until tomorrow," Matt said. "You'll see."

He could hardly wait. Tomorrow was going to be the best day he'd had since he moved to Healy.

Merry Monahan was tall and tanned, with curly black hair. She smiled and waved at the students and teachers who had crowded into the gym to hear her speak.

"I wanted to bring my pets," she said, "but I didn't think Matthew Barber's mother would like it." She winked at Matt as if they were old friends, though they'd met only a few minutes ago. "I'm going to stay at Matthew's house tonight," she went on, "and I don't think an Irish wolfhound and a boa constrictor would be welcome."

Everyone gasped, and Jason poked Matt in the ribs. "What's an Irish wolfhound look like?" he asked.

Matt didn't know. "It's big," he whispered.

Last night, he'd tried to find out more about their houseguest, but his mother had been too busy to talk. She'd put brand-new sheets on the guest room bed, and smelly pink soap in the bathroom, and Matt had to pick a bouquet of daisies for the bedside table. Dinner tonight was going to be lobster tails.

"I'd write a book myself if it meant we could have lobster once a week," his dad joked. "But I guess Matt is going to be the writer in this family. When are we going to read your story, son?"

"After the assembly," Matt had told him.

"What's it about?"

Matt's mother had switched off the vacuum cleaner to listen.

"It's called 'The Ghost in Room Eleven,'" Matt said.

"Oh, my, more wild make-believe!" his mother exclaimed. "First Hollywood stuntwomen and treasure hunters, then ghosts."

Now, sitting on the gym floor, Matt wondered how Merry Monahan and his mother had become friends. They were very different. Miss Monahan said she liked to write about unusual places. She'd slept in a tent in the African jungle and had climbed mountains. She had even driven a dogsled in Alaska.

Matt's mother always said that if a vacation didn't include a clean bed every night and a private bathroom, she wasn't interested in going.

When Miss Monahan finished speaking, Mr. Beasley told her the students had a treat for her. They had been writing stories themselves, and two of them had been chosen to read their work.

Jennifer Berman, a sixth grader, read first. Her story was about what it might be like to be the first sixth grader to ride in a space shuttle. When the story ended Matt clapped with everyone else, though he'd heard hardly a word. He was so excited, he couldn't sit still.

"And now we have Matthew Barber," Mr. Beasley announced.

"His story is called—" He stopped, and Matt could tell he hadn't read the title before. "It's called 'The Ghost in Room Eleven.'" The principal gave a funny little cough and handed the story to Matt.

Matt hadn't thought about what it would be like to stand up in front of so many people. His voice shook as he read about hiding in the closet and being scared by the gerbils. The students giggled. They'd heard that part of the story before, from Charlie.

"'Then I ran upstairs,'" Matt read on in a stronger voice, "'and I saw this weird light at the end of the hall. A lady in a black dress sort of drifted out of Room Eleven. She had a spooky white face, and her eyes just burned into me. She wanted me to come closer, but I didn't. I ran out of there as fast as I could. I never stopped till I got home, even though I heard some kids laughing and wondered if they'd played a trick on me.'"

Matt stole a quick look at Charlie and Jason. He could tell they were remembering that evening, too.

"'The next day I saw the picture of Miss Edna Whipple in the hall,'" Matt continued. "'That was when I knew who the ghost was.'" He took a deep breath and turned a page. The scariest part was still to come.

"'A couple of weeks ago we had a sleep over in the gym,'" he read. "'Miss Carey asked me to get a video from her classroom. It was Room Eleven. I looked through the door, and the ghost was on the other side of the glass. I was so scared that I ran all the way back to the gym. I told Miss Carey I couldn't find the video, so she went to get it herself. I guess she didn't see the ghost. I'm the only one who sees her, and I don't know why.'"

Matt put down his paper, and the students cheered and clapped. He looked at all the excited faces and knew he'd done what he meant to do. Every single student in the gym was wondering if he'd really seen a ghost.

Miss Monahan returned to the microphone. "Both of these stories are very good," she said. "Matthew's story is fun because he wrote about school—a place he knows and you know. He put his imagination to work, and he came up with a good idea." She smiled at Matt. "How did you happen to make up a ghost story, Matthew?"

Matt stared at her in dismay. She was spoiling everything!

"I didn't make it up," he said loudly. "I really saw the ghost!"

"Now, Matthew," Miss Monahan said, still smiling, "it's important to know the difference between what's real and what isn't. We all like your story, whether it's make-believe or not."

"But it *isn't* make-believe," Matt shouted. *"It isn't!"*

"Matthew!" Mr. Beasley jumped up. "That's enough!"

But Matthew couldn't stop. "I'm telling the truth!" he roared. "I am. And I saw the ghost again! I saw her yesterday afternoon. I thought it was Mrs. Sanders standing next to my desk, but

it was Miss Whipple. I saw her, and I *heard* her. She pointed to my paper and she said, 'Shocking!' She was mad at me."

"So am I!" Mr. Beasley bellowed. His face was tomato-red. "Matthew Barber, you sit down right now!"

11

Trouble at Home

"YOU'RE GOING to do *what?*" Matt's mother stopped in the middle of the patio and stared at Matt and Merry Monahan. She had come home early and greeted their guest with a big smile. The smile was gone now.

"We're going to have a ghost hunt," Miss Monahan repeated gaily. "Tonight. At the school."

"But that's nonsense!" Matt's mother exclaimed.

Matt shrank back in his chair.

"It was just a big fuss-and-feathers." Miss

Monahan giggled. "Matthew said he's seen a ghost in the school, and that upset Mr. Beasley."

"I should think so!" Matt's mother sat down.

"It was all my fault," Miss Monahan went on. "I argued with Matthew in front of his classmates, and the children got excited, so I tried to think of something that would satisfy everybody and I suggested—"

"A ghost hunt." Matt's mother shook her head.

"It'll be an adventure," Miss Monahan said bravely. "If we don't see a ghost, Matthew and everyone else can forget the whole thing. If we do see a ghost—" she grinned at Matt "—I'll admit that Matthew was right and I was wrong."

"I can't believe Mr. Beasley would agree to such a thing," Matt's mother said.

"He didn't have much choice, I guess," Miss Monahan said. "When I suggested it, the kids started cheering, and the only way to calm them down was to agree. It's just for fun," she added. "No harm done."

"But it encourages Matthew to lie," his mother said.

"I didn't lie," Matt said softly. He hated grown-ups' arguments, especially when they were arguing about him. It was a relief to hear footsteps around the side of the house. A moment later, his father came out on the patio.

"Good to have you here," he said, after he and Merry Monahan had been introduced. "I bet you two have been having a great time talking over your school days."

Matt's mother stood up. "We've been talking about Matt's school days, not ours," she said crisply. "And I don't much like what I hear. I think I'll go inside and get dinner on the table." She hurried away.

"We're in trouble," Miss Monahan said.

Matt's dad nodded. "I can see that."

He listened while Merry Monahan explained again about the ghost hunt.

"What do you say, Matt?" his dad asked, when she'd finished. "If you don't see a ghost tonight, will you admit it was a good story and that's all it was?"

Matt twisted a button on the arm of his chair. He wanted to prove he was telling the truth, but maybe Miss Monahan's ghost hunt wasn't the right way to do it. The ghost might not show up, if anyone but Matt was there.

"It wasn't just a good story. It really happened," Matt said, for what seemed like the millionth time.

His dad sighed.

"Dinner's ready," his mom called through the kitchen window. "Wash your hands, Matthew."

Her voice was cheery now, but Matt knew she was still angry. There was only one thing that would make her feel better, and that wasn't likely to happen. She would have to see Miss Whipple herself.

12

The Ghost Hunt

MR. BEASLEY WAS JUST pulling into his special parking place when Matt and Merry Monahan started across the playground. Miss Monahan carried a flashlight that sent a bobbing yellow light ahead of them.

"There's a whole bunch of kids at the door," Matt said unhappily. "It was supposed to be just Charlie and Stephanie."

"They are the only ones who'll go inside with us," Miss Monahan said. "You can't blame the others for wanting to get in on the fun."

Matt didn't answer. The ghost hunt was feeling less fun every step he took.

By the time he and Merry Monahan reached the school's door, Mr. Beasley had shooed away everyone but Stephanie and Charlie. He unlocked the door.

"You know I don't approve of this," he said stiffly. "I hope that after tonight we won't hear any more about this ghost business."

"I don't think you will." Miss Monahan smiled at him. "We'll report in the morning."

Mr. Beasley nodded and left them standing just inside the door. Matt watched him march back to his car and wished he were leaving, too.

"Well, Matthew," Miss Monahan said in a low voice. "You're the boss. What do you want us to do?"

Matt looked down the hallway. Two dim lights had been left on between the front door and Room 11. The rest of the hall was filled with shadows.

"You'd better stay here," he said. "Miss Whipple might not come if she sees other people around."

"Suits me," Charlie said promptly. Stephanie, standing close to Miss Monahan, looked relieved.

"I'll walk down the hall," Matt said. "Maybe she'll appear right away, and you'll all see her. If she doesn't—" he had to force himself to say the words "—I'll wait at the end of the hall until I see her."

Charlie shuddered and Stephanie whispered, "Good luck!" She and Charlie hid just inside a classroom, where they could peek around the door frame. Miss Monahan stood in the entrance to the principal's office.

Matt walked stiffly, his fists clenched. He didn't know what to hope for. He never wanted to see Miss Whipple again. Not ever! But if she didn't show herself tonight, everyone would think he was a liar.

If she comes, I'm going to ask her why she's picking on me, he told himself. And then he felt dizzy at the thought of talking to a ghost!

Halfway down the hall, he stopped. *Come out now*, he begged silently. *Don't make me get any closer.*

The hall remained empty. He started walking again. *Now*, he thought. *Now. Now. Now.* But the silvery cloud did not appear.

Just before he reached the door to Room 11,

Matt stopped once more. He couldn't make himself look through the glass panes in the door. He couldn't bear it if Miss Whipple were waiting again on the other side of the glass. Besides, what good would it do if he were the only one who saw her? She *had* to come out in the hall.

For what seemed a very long time, Matt stood there, close to the door, still as a statue. His chest ached. He felt sweaty and cold at the same time.

"Matthew!"

Matt gave a squeal of terror before he realized it was only Merry Monahan who was calling him.

"Come on back, Matthew. Nothing's going to happen."

As soon as she said it, Matt knew she was right. Miss Whipple was angry. She wouldn't help him by letting herself be seen for even one second. He turned and walked back to where the other ghost hunters were waiting.

"Don't look like that, Matthew," Miss Monahan said. "It isn't the end of the world. We all know you *thought* you saw a ghost. And we've had an adventure, haven't we?"

For once, Charlie didn't tease. "I don't think

there is a ghost," he said. "But I wouldn't have walked down there by myself, that's for sure."

"Let's go home," Stephanie said.

Charlie pushed open the heavy door and they filed out into the moonlight. Matt didn't know what to say. He wished he'd taken his parents' advice and written a story about what it was like to be the new kid in school.

Angrily, he pushed a swing as he went by, and then almost fell as his jacket sleeve caught on a chain. When he straightened up he was facing the school.

Miss Whipple stood at the front door in a pool of silvery light.

"Look!" Matt shouted. "Hey, look! There she is!"

The other ghost hunters whirled around and stared. The doorway was dark.

"Oh, Matt, stop acting silly!" Stephanie exclaimed. She sounded as if she was tired of him and his ghost.

"She was right there," Matt insisted. He stared at the empty doorway. Good old Miss Whipple! She'd come back just long enough to help him lose the only friend he had in Healy Elementary!

13

Bad Days Ahead

"ATTENTION! Attention, students!"

Mr. Beasley stood in front of the office loud-speaker with Merry Monahan and Matt behind him.

"Miss Monahan is here to report on last night's so-called ghost hunt here in our school." Mr. Beasley sounded happier, now that the ghost hunt had failed.

Miss Monahan moved up to the microphone and smiled kindly at Matt.

"Matthew and Stephanie and Charlie and I had an adventure," she said. "We didn't see the ghost, but we all thought Matt was very brave when he went looking for her. We shivered and shook because his story had made her seem real. I want to congratulate him again on his terrific imagination. I'll see all of you next week, when I come back to sign books at your Book Fair. 'Bye!"

Matt's face burned. Now all the students thought they knew the truth. Matt Barber made up stories and pretended they were true.

"You may go now, Matthew," Mr. Beasley said. "I trust we won't hear any more about your ghost."

"No, sir." Matt said good-bye to Merry Monahan and walked slowly back to his room. Of course he wouldn't talk about the ghost again. How could he? But he knew his classmates would have plenty to say.

The next few days were as bad as he'd expected. Jason dropped a picture on his desk of a boy with his hair standing up straight as a tall, skinny ghost sneaked up behind him. Kids snickered and shouted "Boo!" at him on the playground. Stephanie said "Hi," every morning but didn't look at him when she said it.

Only Charlie was a surprise. He didn't talk to Matt, but he didn't make fun of him, either. Matt remembered that Charlie had said he wouldn't have walked down the hall to Room 11 by himself. Maybe that was why he was keeping quiet now.

"Matthew, quit moping," Mrs. Sanders said one morning in a soft voice. "Forget about your ghost story and work hard. That's what you're in school for." She must have called his parents again, because that night he got advice from them, too.

"I'm sorry you're having a bad time at school, Matthew," his mother said. "But you really did bring it on yourself, didn't you? From now on, don't forget what's real and what isn't."

"Just laugh it off, Matt," his father said. "A month from now, nobody will remember."

A month! A month was forever! He told himself there must be a way to prove the ghost was real. If he knew why she haunted him, maybe he could figure out a way to make her show up when other people were around.

He had to talk to her. He thought about that in bed and pulled the covers up over his head. He thought about it at school and got all the words wrong on that day's spelling test.

I'll have to hide in the basement again and wait for everyone to go home. Just the thought of it gave him goose bumps. But it was the only way.

14

"I'll Haunt You Forever!"

THIS TIME THERE WERE no gerbils. Matt sat on a box and tried to tell himself he wasn't as frightened as he'd been the first time he hid in the closet. It was no use. The first time he hadn't really believed there was a ghost in Healy Elementary. Now he knew there was.

He opened the door a crack and squinted at his watch in the faint light from the stairwell. Only half an hour had passed since he'd slipped out of line and sneaked down the steps. He made his way back to the box.

He closed his eyes and tried to imagine what he'd be doing if he were back in Milwaukee. Playing ball at the park, probably. He'd told Charlie that he went swimming in the school pool every afternoon, but there was no pool. Matt groaned. He'd told so many stories since he started at Healy Elementary that he couldn't remember them all. It wasn't so surprising that now, when he really *needed* someone to believe him, no one would.

After another long wait, he opened the door again. His watch said five o'clock. He tiptoed to the foot of the stairs and listened. There wasn't a sound.

He started up the stairs on tiptoe. At the top, he looked quickly up and down the hall. Room 11 seemed very far away.

Get going! he ordered himself. He started down the center of the hall. In his favorite western movie, the hero walked alone like this, down the middle of a street, to meet the killer. But Matt didn't feel like a hero. He was terrified.

When he reached the door to Room 11 he took a deep breath and peeked through the glass. Miss

Whipple wasn't there! Matt was relieved and sorry at the same time. If she wasn't in Room 11, he didn't know where else to look.

Trembling, he turned the doorknob. From inside the room came a low, angry muttering. He gave the door a little push and looked inside. Miss Whipple was at the teacher's desk at the back of the room.

"There you are, Matthew Barber." Her grating whisper was all around him. "You are a bad boy!"

Matt wanted to run but didn't. Miss Whipple was talking, and he had to listen.

"You brought people to look at me, as if I were *peculiar!* That writer and her silly ghost hunt! I have almost decided not to save you."

"Save me!" Matt's voice was a startled squeak.

"Of course, save you," the ghost repeated. "I've never known anyone who needed saving more."

Matt tried to guess what she meant. "Do you mean because I don't have any friends?"

"Yes, that's what I mean," she snapped. "Stop lying and losing your temper, you silly child. And you have another problem, too. Good heavens, boy, *you can't spell!*"

With the last three words, the whisper turned into a windy roar. Matt nearly jumped out of his sneakers.

"It's people like you who won't let me rest in peace!" Miss Whipple bellowed. "People who won't try! Did you know the governor of this state can thank me for learning how to multiply and divide? And your teacher—she was too shy to speak above a whisper. And your librarian didn't like to read! As for Mr. Beasley, he was a dreadful speller—as bad as you!" She glared at Matt. "None of them wants to remember me now, of course. They'd like to think they did it all by themselves!"

"How—did you save them?" Matt stammered. He knew he wasn't going to like the answer.

Miss Whipple stood up. She unfolded and stretched until her head touched the ceiling. Her fierce eyes held Matt so he couldn't move.

"I scared them!" she roared. *"I warned them that if they didn't change, I'd haunt them forever! And that's what I'm telling you, Matthew Barber! Try hard, and then try harder!"*

The words ended in a shriek, as the ghost strode

across the room. Matt stumbled, and when he scrambled to his feet, Miss Whipple was almost on top of him, her long arms reaching.

"Go away!" Matt shouted. He tore down the hall with the ghost right behind him. A bone-chilling wind pushed him along, and he could feel Miss Whipple's fingers plucking at his shoulders.

"Matthew Barber," she shrieked, *"I'm going to haunt you forever and ever!"*

Matt hit the push bar of the front door and hurtled out on the playground. Gasping for breath, he risked one quick look over his shoulder.

The big glass door was closed and dark.

15

Two Miracles

"I'M SURE YOU HAVE a fever," Matt's mother said. "You're sweating, and you look strange." She turned to Matt's father. "Don't you think he looks strange?"

"No more than usual," his dad teased. "Since when is doing homework a sign that he's sick?"

Matt hardly heard them. He had just finished writing today's misspelled words ten times. Now he was getting ready for tomorrow's test, and he was writing each word twenty times. His stubby pencil flew down the page.

"Well, I think you're overdoing it," his mother said. "You'd better go to bed early tonight."

"Soon as I finish this," Matt mumbled.

He felt safer with his parents close by, but he couldn't stop thinking about the ghost. She'd be waiting for him tomorrow, and the day after. There would be one spelling test, then another, and if he didn't get all the words right. . . .

"You see, you're shivering," his mother said. "Finish what you're doing and go to bed."

Fifteen minutes later, Matt dropped his pencil and stretched his fingers.

"Good," his mom said. "Now how about a nice snack to make up for the dinner you didn't eat?"

Matt looked out into the dark kitchen. Through the window he could see the deeper dark outside.

"Somebody's there," he quavered. "Looking in at us."

His dad went out into the kitchen.

"Looking in where?" he demanded.

Matt pointed at the window above the sink.

"That's crazy, boy." His dad peered out the window. "A person would have to be ten feet tall to look in." He closed the curtains and came back to the dining room.

Ten feet tall! Matt thought. *No problem.* He glanced nervously at the dining-room windows.

"Matthew, go to bed this minute," his mother said. Matt could tell she was worried about him.

He was worried, too.

The first thing he did in his bedroom was to pull down the shades. Then he undressed fast, put on his pajamas, and jumped into bed, pulling the covers up to his nose. He was sure he wouldn't sleep, but luckily he had a new book about the Little League. He decided to read all night.

An hour later he heard his mother coming down the hall to check on him. Quickly, he shoved the book under the covers and closed his eyes. She felt his forehead and turned out the light. The minute she left the bedroom, he turned the lamp back on.

Maybe, he thought, he didn't have to worry about Miss Whipple at home. He wasn't *sure* he'd seen her at the kitchen window. Maybe she stayed in Healy Elementary. But that was bad enough.

At least now he knew why she was haunting him. She thought he was a mess! Since when was spelling the most important thing in the world? And she'd said he could make friends if he'd stop lying and losing his temper. What did *she* know? How could she think it was his fault no one was friendly in this hick school?

Stop calling it a hick school.

Matt knew the voice was inside his head, but it sounded very much like Miss Whipple's eerie whisper. He pulled a pillow over his face.

The next day Matt was the last person to go through the school door when the bell rang.

"Where were you, Matthew?" Mrs. Sanders asked when he slid into his seat.

"Out looking for a ghost," Charlie said, before Matt could reply. Everyone laughed, and Matt grimaced. Then he thought about what Miss Whipple had said. He swallowed hard, and laughed, too.

"Ghosts show up better after dark," he told Charlie.

To his surprise, Mrs. Sanders smiled approvingly. Later that morning, when he scored one hundred on the spelling test, she clapped her hands.

"Well done, Matthew!" she said. "I'm proud of you."

Matt sighed. One hundred was a miracle. So was Charlie's invitation to shoot hoops after school. But two miracles in one day didn't stop him from being scared. He stayed close to the other students during the lunch hour, and he was the first one on the playground after school. Miss Whipple was around somewhere, he knew, just waiting for him to make a mistake.

16

A Celebration

"WHO WANTS TO GO OUT to eat?" Matt's mother asked gaily, as she put down the telephone. "That was Mrs. Sanders. She called to tell us how well Matthew is doing. Five perfect spelling tests in a row!"

Matt's father fell back in his chair. "It's too much!" he groaned. "I can't stand the shock!"

Matt grinned but didn't look up from his paper. He'd written *escape* fifteen times and had five more to go.

"You'll have to stop studying long enough to eat," his mother said. "Where should we go?"

"Mega-Burger," Matt said at once. It was the only fast-food restaurant in Healy, and the hamburgers were great. He pushed his paper aside. He'd finish tomorrow's list when they came home.

"Whom do we thank for all these perfect scores?" Matt's father asked as they drove across town. "Besides you, of course, Matt. Sounds to me as if Mrs. Sanders should get a medal."

Matt shrugged.

"Matthew just needed time to settle down," his mother said. "He has a good brain when he doesn't clutter it up with silliness. I just hope that next week. . . ."

She didn't finish the sentence, but Matt knew what she was thinking. On Friday of next week Merry Monahan was coming back to sign books at the Book Fair.

"Is Miss Monahan going to stay at our house again?" he asked.

"No, she'll be in town for only a few hours," his mother replied. "I'm going to take the afternoon off and meet her for lunch before she visits the school."

As they turned in at the Mega-Burger parking lot, Matt saw Charlie and Jason at the bike rack. They looked at the Barbers' car, turned away, then looked again and waved. Matt waved back.

"Pals of yours?" his dad asked. "Should we ask them to join us?"

Matt shook his head. The boys had been friendly enough when they shot hoops, but they hadn't invited him to play again. It was as if they were still trying to make up their minds how they felt about him.

Who cares? he thought angrily, and then cringed as the answer sounded inside his head in an eerie whisper.

You do!

Three spelling tests later, Matt still hadn't made a mistake. He worked hard every night, and when he went to sleep he dreamed of Miss Whipple. Sometimes she was in his closet; once he dreamed she came bursting out of his locker. He hoped she knew about his spelling tests.

On the Tuesday before the Book Fair there were no gym classes. Tables and shelves were set up along the gym walls, and there were boxes of books piled in the middle of the room. Posters lined the walls.

"Look in the art room," Stephanie told him, pointing across the hall. "Mr. Beasley is helping, too. He's painting a sign."

Matt looked and then hurried into his classroom. He didn't want to linger in the hallway for even a minute.

That afternoon Miss Bucher came in, waving a sheet of green paper. "This is the invitation to the Book Fair," she said. "You'll each receive one to take home to your parents. But first I need help getting them ready."

Stephanie and her best friend Kristin raised their hands.

Miss Bucher looked pleased. "Now some boys," she said. "How about you, Matthew? Don't you want to help us get ready for your friend Miss Monahan's visit?"

"Okay," Matt said. But he didn't think Miss Monahan was much of a friend. She had practically called him a liar when she told the school about the ghost hunt. It was mostly because of her that he couldn't talk about Miss Whipple to anyone.

Charlie put up his hand, and Jason did, too. "We can help during math class tomorrow," Charlie said, looking sideways at Mrs. Sanders.

Miss Bucher laughed. "Nice try, Charles," she said. "But we're going to work on the invitations this evening. Be here at six, and tell your parents I'll see that you all get home safely."

Charlie and Jason looked disappointed, but Matt stared at the librarian in horror. This evening! He would never have said okay if he'd known it would mean coming back to school in the evening. Goose bumps popped out on his arms.

17

"You Could Be Killed!"

STEPHANIE, Kristin, Charlie, and Jason were waiting at the school door when Matt crossed the playground at six o'clock. By the time he reached them, Miss Bucher's red sedan had pulled into the parking lot.

"Is everybody here?" She unlocked the glass door. "Come inside, then. If we work hard, this won't take long."

She switched on a light, and Matt looked around quickly. The hall was empty.

"You wait here," Miss Bucher said. "I'm going

to the library to get the invitations. We'll work in the art room."

She hurried down the hall, leaving the helpers outside the art-room door.

"This is spooky," Kristin said. "It's so quiet. Except for the wind."

"What wind, goofy?" Charlie scoffed. "There isn't any wind tonight."

"Yes, there is," Stephanie said uneasily. "I can hear it."

They stood very still and listened. The sound of the wind, just a whisper at first, was growing louder. Matt took a step toward the door. *Time to get out!* he thought, but he couldn't run away and leave the others.

"It's coming from the gym," Jason said excitedly.

He ran to the gym door and threw it open. Charlie, Stephanie, and Kristin crowded around him, with Matt in the rear.

An amazing sight met their eyes. Posters, book jackets, and order blanks were flying through the air like giant butterflies. An icy gale scooped up everything light enough to fly.

"What's happening?" Kristin shrieked.

They crowded through the door, only to be slammed against the wall by the wind.

Matt clung to the door frame. This was Miss Whipple's work. He was sure of it.

"Look!" Stephanie pointed up to the ceiling where a long sign flapped on a rope strung from one side of the gym to the other. "That's Mr. Beasley's sign!" she exclaimed. "It's going to be wrecked!"

The fierce wind wrapped the sign around the rope.

The wind's coming from up there, Matt thought. *Right around the sign. But why. . . .*

The sign twisted again, and for a second it hung straight. In that second, Matt knew why the wind was blowing.

"The Book Fair's being spoiled!" Stephanie cried. She tried to catch a book jacket as it sailed past.

Matt looked around frantically. Nearby, a long ladder lay on its side against the wall. Mr. Beasley must have used it to put up his sign.

"Help me!" he shouted. He ran to the far end of

the ladder and started to lift it. Charlie hesitated and then came to help. Together, they braced the ladder against the wall.

"Why?" Charlie yelled, but Matt didn't stop to explain. He had to hurry, or Stephanie would be right. The whole Book Fair would be spoiled.

"Need something sharp," he shouted. Stephanie, looking close to tears, struggled to a table and found a pair of scissors.

"Hold the ladder steady!" Matt shouted. "I'm going to cut down the sign."

Charlie stared at him. "That's crazy," he shouted. "You could be killed!"

Matt started up the ladder. The wind ripped at his clothes and his eyes burned. When he looked down at his classmates, their faces were white with fear. But they all had their hands on the ladder, holding it steady.

He clutched the rungs so hard his fingers ached. He was climbing into the heart of the wind. If he loosened his grip even a little, he would be swept away.

Carefully, he wrapped his left arm around the ladder and reached toward the rope with his right. One more step and he'd be able to touch it. He moved up to the next rung and took the scissors from his pocket. He was shaking so hard that he could hardly close the blades around the rope. Nothing happened. Mr. Beasley had used a heavy rope to make sure his sign wouldn't fall.

Matt closed his eyes and tried again. This time the blades closed firmly on the rope. The ladder swayed as he squeezed the scissors, and for a moment he was sure he was going to fall. Then the rope parted with a *crack*, and the big sign swooped downward.

In an instant, the roar of the wind began to fade. By the time the sign lay on the floor, the gym was silent. Matt scurried down the ladder as book jackets and scraps of paper floated around him.

When he stepped off the ladder, Charlie grabbed his arm.

"What happened?" he demanded. "What's going on?"

Matt couldn't speak. He pointed at the sign lying face down on the floor.

"So you cut down the sign," Jason said in a quavering voice. "But what stopped the wind?"

The door opened and Miss Bucher came in. "What on earth—" She dropped the box she was carrying.

"What's going on here?" she demanded, when she caught her breath. "What have you done— and what's happened to Mr. Beasley's sign?"

Matt took a deep breath and walked over to the sign. He turned it over, hoping the wind wouldn't start blowing when he did so. But the gym remained silent as they all stared at the huge red letters

WELLCOME

Miss Bucher's mouth dropped open. "Why, it's—it's—"

"It's spelled wrong," Matt said.

He ought to know. *Welcome* had been on today's spelling list. He'd written it last night, twenty times.

18

Cleaning up the Mess

"BUT WHAT MADE IT fall?" Miss Bucher wanted to know. "I've been setting things up in here all day. . . ."

The children glanced at each other. "There was this big wind," Stephanie said timidly. "It was blowing everything around and twisting the sign and—"

"A big wind? In the *gym?*"

"That's right!" Charlie said excitedly. "But it stopped when Matt cut down the sign."

"But why?" Miss Bucher seemed dazed. "I don't

understand. Why did you cut down the sign, Matthew? Climbing that ladder was a dangerous thing to do."

Matt wondered if Miss Whipple were hiding close by, listening. She must have been furious when she saw the misspelled sign. After all, Mr. Beasley was one of the people she had "saved."

"Well," Miss Bucher said impatiently. "Why?"

Matt tried to think of an answer. "I had to," he said. "The wind was blowing from up there near the ceiling, and I saw that the sign was spelled wrong, so I thought—I thought I'd better cut it down."

He waited for Miss Bucher to ask "Why?" again, but she didn't. She looked at him hard, and then she nodded, as if she were beginning to understand and didn't want to talk about it anymore.

"Well, whatever happened, we have a lot to do here," she said. "Matt, you and Charlie roll up that sign and take it—" she paused "—take it to Mr. Beasley's office. Stephanie and Jason and Kristin, you and I will pick up papers and tape the posters back on the walls. Let's get busy."

For the next half hour everyone gathered book

jackets, taped posters, and sorted the papers that were scattered around the gym. Then they went to the art room to work on the invitations.

Charlie and Jason sat on either side of Matt while they put READ A BOOK stickers on the invitations. Stephanie and Kristin put the letters into envelopes.

"Why'd you do it, Barber?" Charlie whispered. "Why'd you cut down that sign? How did you know that would make the wind stop blowing?"

Matt had promised himself he wouldn't talk about the ghost again, and he didn't. It was enough to have Charlie and Jason looking at him as if he were a hero. That felt *good*.

"I wanted to get it down because it was spelled wrong," he said carefully. "I didn't know for sure what would happen afterward."

Stephanie and Kristin leaned across the table to listen. "I wouldn't have climbed up the ladder in that wind," Kristin said. "I hate high places."

"So do I," Matt said honestly. "I was shaking!"

As he put a sticker on the last invitation, he realized that, for the first time, he wasn't in a hurry to get away from Healy Elementary.

19

The Ghost Appears

"Do you want to go to Milwaukee with me tomorrow?" Matt's dad asked Friday morning. "I have to work for an hour, but after that we can take in the zoo."

"I can't," Matt said. "I told Charlie I'd play softball. It's a big game."

His parents looked at each other across the breakfast table and smiled. "Some other time, then," his dad said. "Mustn't let the team down."

Matt wondered if they'd be as pleased if they knew about his adventure in the gym. Matt hadn't told them about it, and he hadn't answered his classmates' questions either. *Just stop lying and losing your temper*, Miss Whipple had told him. If he said a ghost had been trying to tear down Mr. Beasley's sign, people would think he was lying again.

Friday afternoon no one felt like working. Mrs. Sanders let the class read the books they'd bought at the Fair that morning. Matt read the first page of his new mystery three times. He wriggled in his seat, wishing the Book Fair were over. He'd be glad when the gym was just a gym again.

"Merry Monahan's here," Charlie whispered from his seat near the window. "She's coming in with a real pretty lady."

Matt sneaked a look. "That's my mom. My *real* mom," he added. "I was kidding about the stunt-woman."

"I know," Charlie said.

A few minutes later Matt jumped as Mr. Beasley's voice boomed over the microphone! "All students report to the Book Fair."

The gym was crowded when the fourth grade

filed in. First, second, and third graders sat on the floor. Behind them were rows of chairs for the fourth, fifth, and sixth graders. In the back sat the parents and grandparents who had come to hear Merry Monahan's talk. Miss Monahan and Mr. Beasley stood on a platform with a microphone and a chalkboard.

"What's the matter with Mr. Beasley?" Jason whispered. "He looks sort of—twitchy."

Charlie snickered and so did Matt. They stopped quickly when the principal scowled at them.

"We're very happy to have Merry Monahan back with us today," Mr. Beasley said. "Let's show her what a nice, quiet audience we can be." He looked at Matt when he said that, as if he were afraid the argument about ghosts might begin all over again.

Matt's face burned. He stared at his shoes while Miss Monahan talked about the books she'd liked when she was a little girl. *Heidi, Treasure Island, Black Beauty, The Secret Garden*—she wrote the titles on the chalkboard. No ghost stories, Matt noticed glumly, but that hadn't stopped her from pretending to be an expert on ghosts.

"And I loved ghost stories," Miss Monahan went on, as if she'd read Matt's mind. She smiled at Mr. Beasley. "Of course," she continued, "we all know there's no such thing as a ghost."

"Right," Mr. Beasley said. "We all know that."

As he spoke, the lights flickered and went out. For a moment light streamed through the small windows high above the floor, and then that faded, too, as if clouds had covered the sun. Everyone began to talk at once. Some of the first graders began to cry.

Mr. Beasley and Merry Monahan were staring up at a corner of the ceiling. Matt turned to look, too, and saw a billowing cloud of silvery mist. He jumped to his feet, ready to run.

"What's going on?" Charlie demanded.

The mist grew brighter. A tall thin figure shimmered into view for a moment, and then, as quickly as it had come, it was gone.

"Hey!" Charlie shouted. "What was that?"

"That was Miss Whipple!" Matt shouted back. "She's proving she's real!"

"Sit down!" bellowed Mr. Beasley. "Everyone please sit down! I believe we have a leaky steam pipe in the ceiling. Nothing to get excited about—"

A beam of yellow light shot out of the mist and lit up the chalkboard behind Miss Monahan. She and Mr. Beasley turned to look at it, and so did everyone else. As they watched, the list of book titles faded, and a message appeared in bold letters:

TRY HARD!

THEN TRY HARDER!

THIS MEANS YOU!

"That's Miss Whipple's motto!" Matt exclaimed. "I told you—she's here!"

The lights came on, and the motto vanished from the chalkboard. When Matt looked back at the ceiling, the silvery mist was gone, too.

"I must be dreaming!" Miss Monahan said to Mr. Beasley, but since she was close to the microphone, everyone heard her. "What in the world happened just then?"

Mr. Beasley didn't answer. His face was gray.

"I want to know what happened," Miss Monahan repeated, sounding frightened. "Tell me!"

"Steam pipe," Mr. Beasley mumbled.

He looked as if he were about to faint.

20

Thumbs up for Miss Whipple

MATT SAT ON A SWING and waited for the rest of the team to show up. He didn't mind being alone on the playground—not much, anyway. After all, Miss Whipple didn't have any reason to be angry with him now. She'd even done him a favor by appearing at the Book Fair. Whether his classmates had seen the ghost or not, they knew something weird had taken place.

He pushed the swing and thought about all that had happened since those terrifying moments in the gym. One thing he'd learned was that grown-ups didn't like to admit they'd been wrong. They hated it!

With the lights back on in the gym, Mr. Beasley had announced in a quivering voice that the Book Fair was over. Students who did not have a book to be signed by Miss Monahan were to go to their classrooms.

Miss Monahan had sat at a table just outside the gym door, smiling as she signed books. But her handwriting was so shaky, it took a long time for Matt to figure out what she'd written in his book:

For Matt Barber,
I still don't believe in ghosts, but someday
I may write a book about a haunted school.
If I do, I'll put a boy named Matt in the story.

Mrs. Sanders had scolded the class for making too much noise on the way back to their room. "The Book Fair's over. It's time to get busy," she'd said firmly. She handed out a new list of spelling words and told Matt to keep up the good work.

Matt's mother wouldn't admit anything unusual had happened, either.

"How was the Book Fair?" his dad asked at dinner last night. "Did everything go smoothly?"

"Merry gave a nice talk," Matt's mom replied quickly. "But then a steam pipe burst in the ceiling and the lights went out, and everyone got excited. It was a huge fuss over nothing."

"A steam pipe put the lights out?" Matt's dad sounded puzzled.

"What about the chalkboard?" Matt demanded. He wondered how his mother could explain that.

She had just shrugged. "I was so far back I couldn't see the chalkboard. I did like the list of books Merry talked about, though. They were ones I read when I was a girl."

Matt dragged a foot to stop the swing. He scooped up a stone and pitched it across the playground. It landed in the teachers' parking lot, next to a crumpled piece of paper.

"Hey, Barber!" Charlie and Jason came around the corner and waved. Matt waved back and then ambled over to Mr. Beasley's place in the parking lot. He picked up the paper and smoothed it out.

FROM THE OFFICE OF THE PRINCIPAL was printed in large letters across the top of the page. Below that were two columns of words in Mr. Beasley's neat handwriting:

WELCOME	WELCOME
WELCOME	WELCOME
WELCOME	WELCOME
WELCOME	WELCOME
WELCOME	WELCOME
WELCOME	WELCOME
WELCOME	WELCOME
WELCOME	WELCOME
WELCOME	WELCOME
WELCOME	WELCOME

Matt grinned and folded the paper. He put it in his jeans pocket. Now he knew there was at least one grown-up who believed the ghost of Healy School was real, even if that person wouldn't admit it.

Without turning around to check, Matt made a thumbs-up gesture, just in case Miss Whipple was watching from a window. Then he ran across the playground to join the rest of the team.